THE PRINCESS
AND THE PEA

ONCE UPON A TIME, THERE WAS A PRINCE WHO DREAMED OF GETTING MARRIED.

TO ACCOMPLISH THAT, HE TRAVELED ALL OVER THE WORLD, BUT HE DIDN'T MEET ANY REAL PRINCESS. SO, HE WAS SAD TO RETURN ALONE TO HIS CASTLE.

ONE NIGHT, A STORM BEGAN WITH LOTS
OF LIGHTNING AND THUNDER.

A PRINCESS, WHO WAS PASSING THROUGH THE PRINCE'S LANDS, SPOTTED THE CASTLE AND DECIDED TO SEEK SHELTER.

THE YOUNG WOMAN WAS GREETED BY THE KING AND THE QUEEN.

SHE SAID SHE WAS A PRINCESS AND THAT SHE HAD BEEN CAUGHT IN THE STORM WHILE RETURNING TO HER KINGDOM. SINCE SHE WAS SOAKED, THE PRINCE'S PARENTS DIDN'T BELIEVE THAT STORY.

THE YOUNG PRINCESS WAS VERY COLD
AND AFRAID OF THE STORM.

THEREFORE, SHE ASKED THE KING AND QUEEN
IF SHE COULD SPEND THE NIGHT IN THEIR CASTLE.

SUSPICIOUS, THE QUEEN WENT TO THE GUEST ROOM, PLACED A PEA ON THE BED, AND ON TOP OF THE PEA, SHE STACKED A PILE OF MATTRESSES.

THEN, SHE OFFERED THE BED FOR THE YOUNG WOMAN TO SPEND THE NIGHT.

THE PRINCESS COULDN'T
SLEEP PROPERLY...

...BECAUSE THE PEA HAD HURT HER BACK ALL NIGHT.

THE NEXT MORNING, THE PRINCESS TOLD THE QUEEN THAT THERE WAS SOMETHING BOTHERING HER IN THE BED. THEN, THE QUEEN WAS CERTAIN THAT SHE WAS A TRUE PRINCESS.

AFTER ALL, ONLY SOMEONE WITH VERY DELICATE SKIN COULD NOTICE THAT THERE WAS A PEA UNDER SO MANY MATTRESSES.

SO THE QUEEN INTRODUCED THE PRINCESS TO THE PRINCE. THEY FELL IN LOVE AT FIRST SIGHT.

THEN, THEY GOT MARRIED AND LIVED HAPPILY EVER AFTER.

THE END